Co

Poems

Poems of a Welsh girl

By

Keely J. Edwards

K.J.E Publishing

Rhythm

Beautiful sounds, endless songs, classical music,

Deep endless souls, searching for love, tender words

put together in a song, magical; an old gentle women,

singing from past. War zones.

Bringing endless memories of sadness, heartache, an

old soul, heart still so young, singing, memories,

with pure love tears falling down her gentle cheeks.

A smile on her fading face.

The love and memories stay deep inside, waiting for

a new day to come, keep singing, keeping the memories

alive for one more day.

Inside the rhythm, it brings the meaning, a song is

so telling, the joy of hearing the piano play,

hearing birds each day in the morning.

She

She brave, no matter how many times her tears roll

down, she still gets back up; her rosy cheeks.

Tearful sad eyes still shine so bright.

"Fake it in till you make it", smile though saddens.

Insecurities, trauma, life, wipe it away.

Make a new day, into something "beautiful".

"She brave" "you're so beautiful", "Put on your boss

smile Girl".

"Be you", "Brave girls", never give up, "Smile more"

"Be free", be Soulful.

She young, She women.

We all know, we all grow.

Chocolate

Delicious mouthfuls of milk chocolate buttons;

Makes the day easier.

Chocolate is sweet and so good to eat, we like it, I like it.

You can have it whenever you like, in the bath, spread

all over your body, lick it up!

Chocolates on a bad day is a winner for Women.

Chocolate Bens and Jerry's ice cream make me scream,

an "orgasm in your mouth".

For Women, dreamy, tasty, just the right amount of

cream on the side.

I like my chocolate like I like my hips.

Journey

We are all just travelers, finding a place or a person

to call home, the feeling of fresh heat, when

you step out of a plane.

Feel the heat on your face, it's going to be a good

day.

Meeting new people from different countries, learning

new languages, seeing the world in a unique way.

Different food, different love, different music.

In a unique way, watching the sunset till late and

gone, singing too music.

So, experience it all.

The world is yours too make, and your make is

your world.

Soulmates

Search and search a million times.

To see the beauty in one person, so many kisses.

"You have to kiss a lot of frogs before you meet your prince."

Tears, sadness, carry on.

Be my soul mate! Lots of love making.

Cook in the evenings, call it home.

Pack lunch ready for morning, on a working day.

The endless fairytale, to last a life time.

Mother

I hope to grow up to be just like my best friend.

The women who loved me from nothing, the woman who gave me everything, my first smile, my first laugh

My first kiss, my first steps.

The endless bond.

A woman's love for her Baby, the women I am today.

Mum, you're not just mum,

You're my shoulder, my nurse when I am ill.

My friend, my hero.

Childhood

Playing in the mud, knees covered with sore cuts,

muddy face with a smile, till you're called in for

tea and bed.

I miss evenings playing tag, I miss my milky pens,

I miss playing Polly Pocket.

The laughter, the fights, the love, the fun.

Waiting for the pop man too come on a Wednesday

and being so happy with my £2 bag of sweets.

The joy of innocents. Chicken stew with the family.

When Mum and Dad had not much money,

putting veg, chicken and potatoes in a pan,

all together to make a memory.

The best sort of memories.

Christmas

Fairy lights on a winter's night.

A child's face, smiling, happy.

The magic feeling.

Christmas is priceless.

Fairytales of New York playing in the background.

Christmas dinner.

Laughing and joyful, the feeling of being surrounded

by your loved ones.

A beautiful day to mark the end.

Tenby

The sun shines so bright, Waves come together

on a windy day. Birds singing.

The harbor, the smell of the chip shop.

Two old souls, side by side on the beach, watching

the waves come apart.

Long walks.

Watching the sunset, the boats coming in, the

boats reaching the shore after a busy day

on Caldey Island.

Children laughing, playing in the sand.

Summer nights by the shore.

Peaceful shore.

Life

A morning hello from a stranger

A Family meal.

A child's hug

A warm cup.

The sounds of the waves.

Seeing a new life come into the world.

Holding hands.

A big table.

"It's not about Money"

A child's voice.

Seeing the world.

Feeling wanted.

Bravery

Bravery is trusting again when trust has failed you.

Bravery is loving again when love has left you.

Bravery is learning to start over.

Bravery is facing trauma.

A chapter in a notepad, a clean sheet of paper.

Brave souls be brave.

For the lessons they teach.

Flowers don't blossom without the will to rise.

Sunshine

Beauty fades but your heart stays the same.

You're my little Miss Sunshine. My heart breaks.

Every time I see you in pain,

But I have to accept life is cruel.

Things come to an end; best friend.

My inspiration, the one who never gave up.

A part of you will always stay.

My little Miss Sunshine.

Through the darkness you saw the light.

You taught me that

I will never give up hope, I will never give up on you.

Because you will always be you.

Glow

Pain makes you stronger.

Believe in the magic of a new beginning.

Smile through the tears, smile through the years.

Let your soul glow.

Broken wings that dare to fly again.

"Show us all your beautiful face"

Because the burning is over.

The fire is done.

Glow amongst the ashes.

Corfu

Greece.

Cocktails in the sun.

Sunny Corfu specials.

"Dance like no one is watching".

Seeing a different culture, the food, the spices.

People in Corfu don't have a lot.

Working for tips for the coming winter to feed there family's.

But at the bar, in the club house, they are happy, happy, happy; Friendly, smiling, no worries in the world.

Dancing to geek music, smashing plates.

The island.

Orange, red, pink colours all mix together

Burning hot sand, clear blue water.

Morning greetings that last till the next.

Addiction

An addiction can ruin your outlook on life.

It takes away pain for a little while.

Emptiness, worthlessness.

But the pain still stays.

Your scars, my hurt still, but it heals in time.

It heals every time you keep climbing, keep moving.

Believe in a new day.

"She is perfect the way she is"

An addictive mind tortured by pain.

The addicted mind plays tricks on innocent souls

You could be a rich man, happy on the outside, but so

lost in the inside, you could be anything in the world.

We are all just humans, trying to find that perfect day.

Winter

The seaside is pure, glowing winter sun.

Windy waves on a rainy day.

Because home is where the waves crash.

Sunday roast, raw laughter, the smallest things.

The autumn magic.

Children's faces, Christmas excitement.

Father Christmas has been.

Joy.

Endless Christmas movies.

Food, a New Year.

A big crowd counting down.

Celebrating.

"Home is where the heart is"

Waves

The wave of life.

Beautiful, even in the bad parts.

A smile can warm these hearts.

Even the strongest have weak points.

Tears are simply raindrops from a storm

inside us. Be strong.

Don't give up on what's best for you.

The wave of life.

Being you is the best thing about you.

Even when life feels like a hurricane.

It's yours hurricane.

Father

The love in my Fathers eyes.

The life he gave to me.

The struggle of making ends meat.

Working nonstop.

Endless hours.

I never went without.

But most of all, I had a hero.

Dad

Showing me the meaning.

"Always have manners".

"Be yourself".

You're with me, my father.

Forever my hero.

Down

Lockdown, the worst is coming.

The struggles are real, the fear is real.

Business is down, money is down, people are

down. Homeless, survival.

Smiles fade to sadness, loneliness creeping in.

War zone, the way back home, Nurses and

Doctors.

Frontline, hands so sore, cry some more.

Some lives are gone forever.

Endless nights and days turn to months.

Breathe, I can't breathe, Breathe.

Body is shutting down, darkness.

There is hope and there is light.

The storm will not last. The sun will

shine at last.

Robins

I never got to see your face, I never got to
hold you,
I never got to embrace your beauty, I never got
to hold your tiny hands
I never got to say, I never got to say.
When robins are near, I know you're close to
us.
Through heartache, through tears.
Through mirrors and years.
I talk about you all the time
Forever in time
So fly like Peter Pan
So we can, so we can.

Lion

Your heart is broken, there is just emptiness;

but

it's also a blessing to feel.

To feel everything so deeply.

To love a curse, to feel pain.

The beauty of pain.

An open wound will heal, so will your tears, so

will the years. Laugh again, be free to love

again, again, again.

You are loved, "love is all around you".

Everywhere you look, see and feel.

When your heart is full.

Don't cry over wolves Be the lion.

Be the fire.

Stretch

Accept your flaws.

Once you accept, no one can use them against you.

"Stretch marks"

Embrace them, they are your tiger-lines, be proud of them.

You made a baby with them; Them, them.

They are part of me, every line, forever mine, forever yours.

I am proud of my life; Wounds.

"I would rather have a body full of scars and a life full of memories".

Face you, face, you, your face, "your face"

I feel worthless.

No one will love a face and body like mine.

Accept yourself, face you.

You again, believe again.

Live

Not everyone has the same heart.

Trust.

"Be loyal but stay true to yourself"

Always be a kind soul, don't let the burden of your

past, pass your future.

We all change.

We all grow up, we all try, we all grow down.

Off in the sky.

Your here for a good time not a long time.

Sitting

Watching the world go by.

Seeing the fisherman catching fish.

Seeing the boats going in and out, the smell of sea

and fish in the air, a summer day, the colours

change.

Every season, the sunset, going down.

Living by the sea.

"That girl that lived by the shore"

Look around some more.

Mothers face, sitting with Nan.

Talking about the 80s "How it was", how it was

for her growing up.

The colours change, change again, again.

Lost

Searching for a place to belong.

"Her mind is blank" "Her mind is full of dreams"

She is just a lost girl searching for a place to exist.

To be.

Forever, souls meet together, stay together, a kind of

love.

Maybe a part of her is still broken, Lost in her own

world.

You're Dreaming.

A happy ending.

"She loves too much"

I'm dreaming, there dreaming, we're dreaming.

Wake up.

To be.

Queen

You're strong, you're god dam sassy baby girl, show it off.

Your confidence, show off your unique style, put on your red lipstick.

Walk with sass, get your glow on girl, put your favorite channel number 5 perfume on.

Walk your flaws, show them off.

You're not like those Women in the magazines.

So don't hide away, my darling girl.

Make them stop and stare, stay true.

For you are a Queen.

Niece

Joy to my heart.

Light to my eyes.

Your smile warms me.

"Auntie"

Aunties can hug you like a mother, keep your

secrets

like a sisters,

And share love like a friend.

Little miss sunshine.

I never felt so proud.

I will forever be there to wipe away your tears.

Through my years, and over my years.

I will be there.

My sunshine.

Moon

The moon reminds me of you.

Beautiful, so far away.

The moon at night, she is peaceful.

She has a side of her, so dark.

She has a side of her, so cold.

The moon knows all your secrets.

The stars shine so bright, looking down, down
on her.

You be the sun, I'll be the moon.

When the night comes

Light back up in the morning

Right next to you.

Printed in Great Britain
by Amazon